NORMAN BRIDWELL
Clifford®
KEEPS COOL

SCHOLASTIC INC.
New York   Toronto   London   Auckland   Sydney

To Eva Moore

The author thanks Manny Campana
for his contribution to this book.

No part of this publication may be reproduced in whole or in part, or stored in a retrieval system, or transmitted in any form or by any means, electronic, mechanical, photocopying, recording, or otherwise, without written permission of the publisher. For information regarding permission, write to Scholastic Inc., Attention: Permissions Department, 555 Broadway, New York, NY 10012.

ISBN 0-439-04394-8

13 14 15 16 17 18 19 20   02 03 04

Printed in the U.S.A.   24

First Scholastic printing, May 1999

607721

Clifford and I can hardly wait until the summer comes.

I hope it's not as hot as last summer.

Last summer we had the hottest weather I can remember. Clifford was really uncomfortable. I made sure he had plenty of water to drink.

He drank all the water in his bowl, but he was still sort of thirsty.

So he drank some more. He just couldn't get cool.

Clifford saw a dog go by in a car. She looked as if she was enjoying the breeze. Clifford is too big to fit in a car.

He saw a truck at a traffic light.

Before I could stop him, he jumped on.

Ah, that felt good. Clifford was enjoying the breeze...

...until the truck came to an underpass. Oh my!

Clifford wasn't hurt, but he was embarrassed.
And he was still hot.

He started to walk back home.

Then he saw some people and their dogs in a swimming pool.

Clifford didn't wait for an invitation.

That was a mistake.

The people were a little upset. Clifford decided to find another way to cool off.

He was passing the arena when he felt
a cool rush of air from the entrance.

He walked around to the side door...

...and squeezed in. The ice looked nice and cold.

Clifford was cool at last.

The ice skaters were angry.

"Get out of here," they said. "You are melting the ice."

Clifford was sorry. He was only trying to get comfortable.

He was leaving when I caught up with him.

I said, "Clifford, I know where you should be on such a hot day."

We headed for the park at the edge of town.

What a wonderful sight — the waterfall!

Now Clifford was comfortable.

Suddenly we heard shouts. Some kids in a boat were in danger.

Luckily, Clifford was right there.

Once more, he saved the day.

The kids' father thanked Clifford. He said
Clifford was a pretty cool dog.

He was right about that.